# *Walking with Mama*

## Barbara White Stynes

DAWN PUBLICATIONS

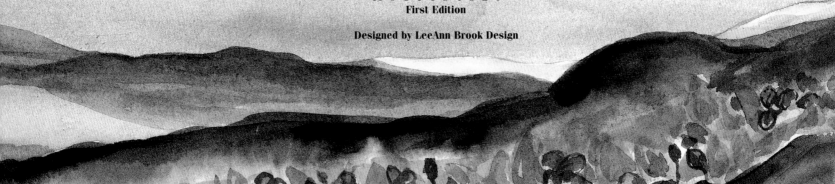

I dedicate this book to my children:
Colin, Kathleen, Evvie and Sean. —*BWS*

Published by DAWN Publications
14618 Tyler Foote Road
Nevada City, CA 95959
916-478-7540

Stynes, Barbara White.
   Walking with Mama / written and illustrated by
Barbara White Stynes. -- 1st ed.
   p. cm.
   SUMMARY: A mother and toddler take a walk in
which they discover the wonders of nature and
deepen the wonders of love.
   ISBN: 1-883220-56-4 (hbk)
   ISBN: 1-883220-57-2 (pbk)

   1. Nature--Juvenile fiction.   I. Title.

PZ7.S896Wa 1997          [E]
                              QBI96-40671

Printed in China

10 9 8 7 6 5 4 3 2 1
First Edition

Designed by LeeAnn Brook Design

My Mama likes
to walk everywhere.

*I* try to walk with her, but her legs are longer and she is stronger.

Mama likes to walk far. When I get tired she carries me in her backpack.

*I* ride up
high where
I can hold her
shoulders.

*I* see the pretty things she sees. Fields of wildflowers meet the far away hills.

Mama walks fast and it is bouncy!
I like moving up and down in the sky.
I try to touch the clouds way up high.

As we walk,
the trees come close
to me. I feel the rough
and smooth bark,
and shiny leaves
that are near.

*I* grab a leaf to hold for my treasure. Mama laughs when the dewdrops fall on us and make us wet.

We stop when we see wild berries along the path. My favorite kind are the juicy red strawberries.

Mama says if I eat too many,
I'll turn into one myself!

Crickets, frogs and grasshoppers talk to us from the tall weeds. The birds sing to us from the tree branches above. I wish I could catch a dragonfly.

The wind blows the cattails in the marsh and pushes Mama's hair against my cheek. I laugh because it tickles.

Mama talks to me about the things we see and find. I rest my head on her shoulder. I can smell the pine trees.

We've been walking
for a long, long time.

*I* hear Mama's breathing, and feel her strong legs moving. The quiet bouncing and Mama's talking make me sleepy.

Many pretty things
pass by me.

*I* try to keep my eyes open,

but the sounds of the river, the colors of the clouds and sky, the wind in the woods and fields, the music of the birds and insects

and the warmth of
Mama's love
all put me to sleep.

Mama's happy
because she can walk
everywhere with me.
I'm happy because
I am with Mama.

## About the Author/Illustrator

Barbara White Stynes has lived in the shadows of the
Rocky Mountains and the Great Smoky Mountains. She
has kayaked and backpacked throughout northern
Michigan, Canada, and the islands of the Great Lakes.
She and her husband, Daniel, have always included
their four children on these adventures, sharing with
them a deep enjoyment and appreciation of nature.
From these many experiences with her own children,
*Walking With Mama* evolved. Barbara resides in Michigan with her family,
where she continues to write and illustrate children's books.

DAWN Publications is dedicated to helping people experience a sense of unity
and harmony with all life. Each of our products encourages a deeper sensitivity
and appreciation for the natural world. For a free catalog, or for information
about school visits by our authors and illustrators, please call 800-545-7475.

J
FIC
Sty

**Wee Read**

Walking with Mama.

DEMCO